DIARY OF AN
ICE PRINCESS

Icing on the Snowflake

For Anna, who worked her
magic on all our books

ISBN 978-1-338-60750-5

2 2020

Printed in the U.S.A. 23

First printing 2020

Book design by Yaffa Jaskoll

DIARY OF AN ICE PRINCESS

Icing on the Snowflake

Christina Soontornvat

Illustrations by
Barbara Szepesi Szucs

SCHOLASTIC INC.

TO HAVE AND TO COLD

☀ SATURDAY ☀

Dear Diary,

   Not having any brothers and sisters can get lonely sometimes. But lucky for me, I have a ton of cousins to make up for it! I love all my cousins so much.

But if I had to pick one cousin I wish I could be like when I get older, it would be Wendy. I have always looked up to Wendy. Like everyone in my family, she has magical weather powers.

She used to babysit me when I was little, and we had the best time playing together. The thing I love most about her is that even though she is also a royal princess, she likes being silly and isn't afraid to get messy.

I never thought someone could be cooler than Wendy. But I was wrong. Because her boyfriend, Sunny, is just as awesome.

Ahem, I mean her *fiancé*, Sunny.

Diary, I am so excited that Wendy and Sunny are getting married! I hope one day they have adorable babies and then *I* will get to be the cool older cousin who babysits.

Claudia was up at our castle having
a playdate today when Wendy, Sunny,
and my great-aunt Eastia flew in. In our
family, it's a tradition for the bride and
groom to deliver wedding invitations by
hand just before the big ceremony.

"Claudia, you and Lina are getting so

big!" said Wendy, giving us hugs. "What happened to the little girls I used to babysit?"

"At least Gusty is still tiny," said Sunny as my puppy covered him in slobbery kisses.

My mom offered to take Great-Aunt Eastia's coat. "Won't you stay and have tea with us?" she asked.

"I'm afraid we don't have time," said Eastia. "We are delivering invitations all over the sky today, and we still have quite a few left."

"We have been flying all morning," Wendy whispered to me. "I need a snack or I'm going to evaporate!"

Eastia cleared her throat and scowled. I love my great-aunt, but she is also very strict about manners.

"What I meant to say is that we would be honored to have you attend our wedding ceremony at Granddad's castle." Wendy and Sunny bowed to my mom and dad, then handed them a thick envelope.

And then they handed one to Claudia!

Claudia gasped. "I'm invited, too?"

"Of course!" said Wendy. "You're just like family, so you have to be there."

Claudia and I bowed very formally to Great-Aunt Eastia. We thanked Wendy and Sunny very politely for inviting us.

We walked very gracefully into the other room.

And then we jumped up and down and started shrieking!

Oh my glaciers, Diary, my best friend and I are going to the royal wedding of the year!

PACK IT UP

This afternoon, Mom and I worked on packing everything we would need for the wedding. I was slightly less excited when I saw what I would have to wear.

"Mom, this dress looks itchy! Can't I wear something more comfortable?"

Packing list:

* Stiff shoes
* Fancy hair barrettes
* Poofy dress
* Even poofier dress

"Trust me, I'd rather wear comfy clothes, too," said Mom. "But a Windtamer wedding is a very formal occasion. It's a tradition to get dressed up."

My dad came in, holding a tuxedo.

"Since I'm a Groundling with no magical powers, can I be excused from this tradition?"

"Nice try," said Mom, tossing him a bow tie.

I caught the bow tie and put it on Gusty. "Now that's what I call a dapper dog. Gusty will be the most handsome guy there."

Mom crossed her arms and raised an eyebrow at me. "Lina, we are going to be on our very best behavior at this wedding."

I sighed. "By 'we,' I know you really mean *me*."

"I'm serious, sweetheart. I know this sounds like fun and Claudia will be there,

but I need you girls to be good listeners
when we're at Granddad's castle. I will
be busy helping Eastia with the flowers,
so you have to promise not to get into
trouble, okay?"

Diary, can you believe Mom even
asked me that? Of course I wouldn't
dream of getting into trouble!

3

A MAGICAL GATHERING

❄ WEDNESDAY ❄

This morning we took Dad's plane down to Earth to pick up Claudia. (We tried to keep the excited shrieking to a minimum, but it was hard.)

Granddad is hosting the wedding

because he has the biggest castle in the sky. When we arrived, I couldn't believe how busy it was! Aunts, uncles, and cousins had flown in from all across the world to attend the wedding. Windtamers and Sparkarchers and Stormstirrers were all swirling about in the castle entrance, laughing and hugging one another. When you get that many magical folks in one room, it can be chaos!

It was hectic, but I loved it. Granddad's castle is usually so empty and quiet. This is the way it should feel all the time—full of family.

There was so much noise that I didn't even notice my granddad until he was right next to us. He's the North Wind and he shouts, so I usually hear him a mile away.

"LINA, IT'S ABOUT TIME MY FAVORITE **GRANDDAUGHTER SHOWED UP!"** He leaned down to whisper in my ear. "I can't say 'favorite' out loud because your other cousins are here." He winked. **"WHY DON'T YOU TAKE CLAUDIA TO YOUR ROOM TO GET SETTLED?"**

Granddad's castle is so enormous. We were out of breath by the time we raced up and up all the stairs to the east wing of the castle.

We jumped on the beds while Gusty snuggled into his pallet. Suddenly we heard a knock at the door and a bloom of frost formed over the window.

A voice in the doorway said, "I thought I saw you guys come in."

"Jack!" It was my other favorite

cousin, Jack Frost. Claudia and I both rushed to hug him.

Jack is a Winterheart, just like me, which means he also has powers over ice and snow. There was a time when we didn't get along, but after he stayed at our castle and went to my school, we

became really close. We've been sending
each other letters to keep in touch.

"I've never been to a wedding
before," I said to him. "Isn't this going
to be so much fun?"

Jack rubbed the back of his neck. "I
guess. But so far, it's been a lot of work.

Dear Lina,
I got your last letter.
Wow, did you really create
a puppy out of snow and
bring it to life? You have
to teach me how to do
that when I visit!
Love, Jack.
PS: The penguins
all say hello.

Princess Lina
Windtamer Castle
The Sky

Just wait—Great-Aunt Eastia is going to put you both to work, too."

"We don't mind. We want to help out. How about Great-Aunt Sunder? Did she come with you?"

I was relieved when Jack said no. He lives with my great-aunt Sunder (the South Wind) down at the icy bottom of the world. Sunder doesn't really get along with the rest of my family.

"She didn't even send a present!" said Jack as he pulled out an envelope from inside his jacket. "But she did send a letter that I'm supposed to give to Great-Aunt Eastia."

"Let's go find her together," I said.

When we got to the stairs, Jack and
I knew just what to do. We called up our
winter magic and iced over the handrail.
Then the three of us slid around and
around, all the way to the bottom!

Diary, I know Jack said the wedding
was a lot of work, but right then it felt
like pure play!

4

A BLAST OF ICY MEANNESS

We found Great-Aunt Eastia with my mom and a bunch of my other aunts in the parlor room, helping Cousin Wendy try on her wedding shoes.

"Are those actual glass slippers?" Claudia asked. "They're so beautiful. You look like Cinderella!"

Wendy teeter-tottered on the glass shoes. "They may look beautiful, but they are impossible to walk in! How am I going to dance in these?"

"Dance?" said Great-Aunt Eastia. "At a Windtamer wedding, the bride and groom do *not* dance. They sit very regally and *watch* the dancing."

Wendy gave me a wow-that-sounds-like-a-real-blast look.

"Great-Aunt Eastia, I have a letter

for you," said Jack, handing her the
envelope from Great-Aunt Sunder.

Eastia scowled as she opened the
letter and read it out loud for the room:

Dear Family,
I regret to inform you that
I shall not be attending the
wedding. But even though I am
not there, you must still uphold
the family traditions and do
your best not to embarrass our
good name.

Mom sighed and rolled her eyes.
"Sunder always did know how to bring
down the mood."

Seriously, what a terrible thing for Great-Aunt Sunder to write!

Great-Aunt Eastia was fuming. She balled the letter up in her hands and crumpled it. "Well, we'll show her! This will be the grandest celebration of tradition that anyone has ever seen. The whole sky will be talking about it for decades!"

Just then we heard barking and Gusty ran into the room. He jumped up into Wendy's arms and started licking her face, which made her laugh. Good old Gusty. He can always tell when someone is sad.

Wendy laughed so much that she

lost her balance on her super-tall glass
slippers. She tumbled over onto the
floor.

Great-Aunt Eastia turned to me.
"Lina! What is that dog doing here?"

"You said everyone in the family was

invited, right? Gusty's a part of the family."

I had thought Gusty could play with Granddad's puppy, Flurry. But Great-Aunt Eastia had taken one look at that gigantic, energetic pup and sent her away to a cloud pasture for the weekend. That meant Gusty was bored and getting into trouble.

"Lina, that dog needs to be locked up," said Eastia. "He is not to come out of your room for the rest of the wedding festivities."

"Yes, Great-Aunt Eastia."

Eastia clapped her hands. "Listen, all of you. We are going to work together to make this the most perfect wedding in the history of Windtamer weddings!"

Somehow, Diary, that didn't sound like much fun at all.

5

REPORTING FOR DUTY

※ THURSDAY ※

Everyone in our family has a job to do for the wedding.

My mom is in charge of the flowers.

Great-Uncle Weston is in charge of the music.

My dad is in charge of making sure
guests know where to go.

My cousin Jack is in charge of making
the table decorations.

Of course Great-Aunt Eastia is in
charge of everything.

And my granddad?

"I AM IN CHARGE OF MAKING SURE EASTIA DOESN'T BLOW HER TOP OVER THIS WEDDING!" he boomed as he paced back and forth in the library. "AND I HAVE TO GIVE A SPEECH, TOO!"

"Granddad, don't you think Claudia and I need a job? I mean, other than just watching over Gusty?"

"I could put together a great playlist of dance songs for the reception," suggested Claudia.

Granddad scowled down at a big sheet of paper. "LINA, CLAUDIA, NOT NOW, PLEASE. I HAVE TO CONCENTRATE!"

"What is that, Granddad?" I asked.

"IT'S THE SEATING CHART FOR THE REHEARSAL DINNER. EASTIA ASKED ME TO APPROVE IT."

"Why do we have to rehearse eating dinner?" I asked. "Doesn't everyone know how to eat?"

Claudia smacked her forehead. "The rehearsal is for the *wedding*. Everyone practices where they will stand during the ceremony. After that, you eat a big dinner to celebrate not having to practice anymore."

"Oh . . ." I said. "Why do you need a seating chart? Can't everyone just sit wherever they want?"

"IT'S TRADITION," said Granddad.

"PERSONALLY, I DON'T CARE WHERE ANYONE SITS! BUT IF I TELL EASTIA THAT, SHE'LL GIVE ME A LECTURE."

Granddad slumped in his chair. I always thought it was funny that big, blustery Granddad is kind of afraid of his tiny little sister, Eastia.

"Granddad, why don't you let Claudia and me take this back to Great-Aunt Eastia and deliver the message that you appreciate her work on this and that you approve."

"THAT IS A BRILLIANT IDEA! THEN I DON'T HAVE TO DEAL WITH HER . . . ER, I MEAN-THEN YOU CAN HAVE A PURPOSE! THAT'S YOUR JOB, LINA. YOU ARE THE OFFICIAL ROYAL FAMILY COMMUNICATIONS OFFICER." He looked at Claudia and smiled. **"CO-OFFICER WITH CLAUDIA, OF COURSE."**

"Yes, sir, Your Majesty, sir!" I said with a salute.

Out in the hallway, Claudia and I smiled at each other. "Communications Officers—now that sounds official!"

"Yup, we are going to need a whole new secret handshake for this!"

6

AS YOU FREEZE

Claudia and I walked to the ballroom, where the rehearsal dinner would be held. By the time we got there, I was ready to rehearse eating a snack!

We found Great-Aunt Eastia sitting at one of the tables, surrounded by hundreds of little paper cards.

"Great-Aunt Eastia, Granddad sent us with a message for you."

"A message?" she asked.

"He says that . . . well, he says that you are so good at doing the seating arrangements that he wants to leave it all in your hands. He trusts you completely."

Eastia smiled and nodded. "Excellent. Then I've made my decisions and we will go with these." She placed the paper cards in neat little stacks. "Now if you'll excuse me, I must go check on the castle chef and see how he's coming along with the wedding cake."

The mention of cake made my mouth

water! But before I could suggest we go get a snack, Claudia and I heard a groan.

My cousin Jack stood at a table in the corner, with his head in his hands. "I am never going to finish these decorations!"

Claudia and I went over to see what he was working on. Jack is so good at doing frost magic—delicate, lacy designs made of ice crystals. "Jack, these are so beautiful," I said. "They're really going to make each table look nice."

"The problem is that there are too many tables! I have to do the exact same thing on each one."

"Ohh, that is a problem. I wish I could help you, but we both know that my magic isn't about making things look pretty and delicate. That's your specialty."

Jack sighed. "Don't worry about it. I'll just work on it all night. Who needs to sleep or take a shower or eat, anyway?"

Claudia snapped her fingers and got a big smile on her face. I knew that look. It was her *I-know-how-to-solve-this-problem* look. "What you need is an assembly line. On an assembly line, each person does their special task and then passes it to the next person to do theirs. It's efficient—that means we won't waste time or energy getting it done."

She explained her plan:

Claudia's plan:

1. Lina swirls up a column of ice.

2. Jack makes pretty frost design.

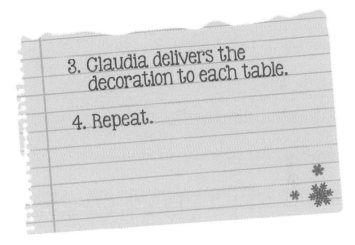

3. Claudia delivers the decoration to each table.

4. Repeat.

I held out my palm and breathed out slowly. My breath formed a solid mass of ice, which I shaped into a column with my fingers. Next, Jack waved his fingers slowly in the air. The air around him chilled and beautiful patterns of frost blossomed all around. With a flick of his fingers, his frost pattern swirled around the ice column.

"Perfect!" said Claudia. "Only thirty more to go!"

I decided to give Claudia a little help. I swooped out my arm, laying a thin layer of ice on the ballroom floor. Why should Claudia have to walk between tables when sliding was so much more efficient?

Pretty soon, Diary, we were rockin' and rollin'. Jack and I were churning out the table decorations, and Claudia was zipping between tables. In practically no time at all we had finished all of them. When we were done, the ballroom looked like a beautiful winter wonderland.

"It just needs one final touch, don't you think?" said Jack with a wink.

He made a cluster of frost crystals. I blew out a deep breath, stringing them together into a glittery frost garland that hung across the room.

"Now *this* looks like a royal ballroom," I said.

"Uh-oh," said Claudia. "I think you may have gotten carried away with all that wintry wind stuff!"

She pointed to Great-Aunt Eastia's pile of seating cards. They were lying all over the floor, completely mixed up!

We rushed to the cards to put them in order again, but it was a total jumbled mess. Suddenly we heard footsteps in the hall outside. Eastia was coming back!

We shuffled the cards together and stacked them on the table.

Great-Aunt Eastia clapped her hands when she came into the ballroom. "Children, this is beautiful!" She

squeezed the three of us in a smooshy hug. "This rehearsal dinner is going to be completely perfect."

Gulp, Diary, I sure hope she is right!

7

SNIP-SNAP

✳ FRIDAY ✳

Only a few family members went to the wedding rehearsal, but everyone was invited to the rehearsal dinner. By this time, Granddad's castle was filled to the top with family from all over the skies. Every Windtamer, Winterheart,

Sparkarcher, and Skypainter was in attendance.

Everyone except Great-Aunt Sunder, of course. Which is funny because even though she wasn't there, I felt like my whole family was trying to impress her.

"Lina, you've got a stain on your dress!" gasped Mom. She spit on a napkin and wiped it all over me. (Ew!) "Don't let your great-aunt Eastia see it. The dinner is about to start and all the guests are here."

"But, Mom, all the guests are our family. They already *know* that I always have stains on my clothes!"

Claudia turned to my mom. "Ms. Gale, how about I take Lina to our room and we'll try to get that stain out?"

My mom nodded. "Thank you, Claudia. Just be back in the ballroom in time for dinner. And, Lina, remember what we talked about—be on your best behavior."

I scratched my legs as we walked back to our room. "Even if you get the stain out, there is no way I can make it through the entire dinner in this dress. It's so itchy!"

My mom had ordered Claudia and me similar dresses in different colors. They were super fancy, and that meant super itchy.

"Don't worry," said Claudia. "I have a plan to de-itch these dresses."

Back in our room, Gusty was whining at the door to be let out.

"Sorry, buddy," I said, scratching his ears. "You are definitely not allowed to go downstairs tonight."

Claudia rummaged through the desk drawer until she found a shiny pair of scissors.

"What are those for?"

"The lacy petticoats under our dresses are the reason we're itching.

They have to go. I'm a whiz with scissors. I've made all my cutoff shorts by myself."

"But are you sure? That sounds so . . . nontraditional"

Claudia fluffed the skirt of her dress. "This thing has a thousand layers! No one is going to notice if we remove just one."

"You're right," I said. "Get snipping."

Carefully, Claudia cut out the bottom layer of petticoat from my dress, then hers. When she was done, I felt so relieved—no more itching!

"Ha-ha, now I know how poor Gusty feels when he finally gets an ear scratch!" I said. "Right, buddy? Um, Gusty?"

We turned and realized that we had left the bedroom door open!

Claudia and I looked at each other. It was the *oh-please-don't-let-this-be-happening* look.

We raced out the door. "GUSTY!"

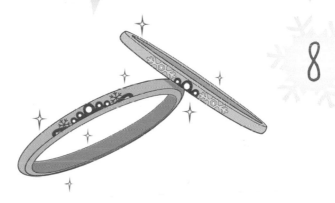

8

REHEARSAL FOR A DISASTER

We searched everywhere for Gusty.
In all his favorite hiding places, under
the stairs, in the hallways. We even
peeked into the library, where Granddad
was practicing his big speech. Still
no pup.

We decided to check the ballroom.

When we got there, we gasped with delight. Oh, Diary, the whole room was so beautiful! The candlelight sparkled in Jack's frosty decorations. The orchestra played softly and people swayed to the music.

But as we walked closer, we realized that they weren't swaying to the music. They were *slipping*.

"Lina, the ice you made on the floor yesterday!" said Claudia. "We forgot all about it!"

Oh. My. Gravy boats.

I clutched Claudia's arm. "I think as Communications Officers, we need to

communicate that we have a disaster on our hands!"

"Right. We need to tell your great-aunt Eastia."

But before we could look for her, she arrived with my granddad in tow.

Great-Aunt Eastia has the power to make warm air, and with a flick of her wrist, the icy floor melted. My granddad snapped his fingers. A powerful gust of wind blew through the ballroom, whisking the melted water away (and messing up some hairdos in the process).

Eastia hurried to the middle of the room, where Wendy and Sunny were standing. "My goodness, are you all right? What a disaster!"

Wendy and Sunny were laughing. "It's fine. It was actually a lot of fun to slide around! It made this a night to remember."

"Well, we can't have any more slipups like that one!" said Eastia. "You'll see, my dear. The rest of this weekend will go perfectly smoothly."

Eastia caught my eye and waved for me to come closer. "Lina, did you have anything to do with the icy floor?" she whispered.

"I'm sorry, Great-Aunt, I can explain . . ."

Great-Aunt Eastia started to give me the Look of Disappointment, but then she glanced around at the tables. "Why is everyone sitting in the wrong spots?"

Oh dear. The seating cards!

Eastia turned to me, flustered. "Lina, your grandfather tells me he gave you the job of message runner. Well, I have an urgent message for you to run. Go to the kitchen and tell our chef that dinner will begin later than planned. Quickly, please!"

Claudia joined me outside in the hall and squeezed my hand. "That was a close one! At least Wendy and Sunny looked like they were having a great time."

"Yes, but I don't think this was the right way to kick off the perfect wedding. And we still have to find Gusty!"

As we headed for the castle kitchen,
I made a solemn vow not to mess
anything else up for the rest of the
night.

9

PUPPY BREATH

When we got to the castle kitchens, the food smelled so good that I nearly forgot all about my assignment!

Chef Rehan was there, overseeing the entire feast. I introduced him to Claudia and he let us try out the appetizers because I am his special taste-tester.

Spicy noodles

Sunset pudding

Steamed dumplings

I had to pull myself away from the
food to remember why we were there.
"Chef Rehan, we came with a message
from my great-aunt Eastia. She says
that dinner will be late."

"Not a problem," said Chef Rehan. "I

will just put the pastries away to cool for now. Claudia, will you please hold open the refrigerator door? Lina, you can help me carry in the dessert trays."

The kitchen has a gigantic walk-in refrigerator. Claudia swung open the big door and then immediately shut it again.

"What is it?" I asked.

She raised her eyebrows and gave me a *do-not-go-into-that-refrigerator* look.

I heard a little yip.

We had found my dog.

I turned to Chef Rehan. "Chef, you have so much to do to prepare. Why

don't you let me and Claudia move all the

desserts into the cooler for you?"

"Well, if you're sure you don't

mind . . ."

I took the dessert tray from him.

"We insist!"

"Why, thank you, girls, that's so nice of you. Just be careful when you get inside. My One Thousand Almonds Cake is in there, and I just finished frosting it for the wedding tomorrow."

Once Chef Rehan turned around, Claudia and I slipped into the refrigerator and shut the door behind us.

Gusty leaped up into my arms.

"Gusty, you naughty little puppy! We have been looking for you everywhere!"

He yipped and licked my face.

Claudia stood behind the massive wedding cake. She looked up at me.

"Uh-oh, I don't think you're going to want to see this, Lina."

"Hold on a second . . ." I said as I held Gusty out at arm's length. "Why does your breath smell like vanilla?"

10

EASY COME, EASY SNOW

"Oh, Gusty, what did you do?"

The backside of the cake had a gigantic hole in it! My little puppy had eaten enough cake to feed a dogsled team.

"Gusty, I think you are going to have a tummy ache tonight," said Claudia.

"Great-Aunt Eastia is going to kill me!" I wailed.

"Shh, Chef Rehan will hear you!" said Claudia. "We need to think fast about how to fix this!"

"But how can we fix it? Chef has been working on this One Thousand

Almonds Cake for two days. He'll never be able to make another one in time for the wedding tomorrow."

Claudia tapped her chin. "At my uncle's wedding, they didn't even eat all the cake. The bride and groom took a slice from the top and then most of it was left over."

I snapped my fingers. "You're right. It just has to *look* perfect for tomorrow. Once the wedding is done, no one will notice if the cake isn't actually perfect, right? We just need to patch up that hole."

Lina reached for a large mixing bowl on the shelf beside her. She dipped her finger inside and licked it. "This is leftover vanilla icing. If you can fill in the hole with snow, we can add frosting over the top and no one will know the difference!"

I held my hands out over the cake and waved them in slow circles. Making snow inside the walk-in refrigerator was easy since it was already so cold inside. I sculpted the snow until it had perfectly filled in the hole that Gusty had eaten. Claudia dipped a spatula into the icing and began smoothing it over the snow patch. When she was done, it looked flawless. You couldn't tell where the real cake ended and the snow cake began.

"Want to lick the spoon?" asked
Claudia.

Gusty yipped.

"No way," I said, scooping him up into
my arms. "You are not getting any sugar
for the rest of the year!"

We slipped out of the cooler and

shut the door behind us. Before we left, I dialed the temperature way down so the snow cake would stay intact until the next day.

We put Gusty in our room and made *triple* sure to lock the door before going back to the ballroom for dinner. By that time, Eastia had sorted out the table cards and everyone was sitting in their proper places. I kept looking at Wendy and Sunny. They smiled through the dinner, but I could tell something was wrong.

They must have been disappointed that the night hadn't gone perfectly.

Well, Diary, I am determined that the rest of the wedding is going to be different.

It's my own personal mission to make this wedding the most perfect wedding of all time!

11

DRESSED TO CHILL

This morning Claudia and I both woke up early without being asked because we are enacting Operation Everything Goes Smoothly. We both took showers and helped each other do our hair.

Then I pulled something out of my

suitcase that I had been keeping as a surprise for this very moment.

"Makeup?" said Claudia. "But are we allowed to wear it?"

"Well, it is a special occasion," I said. "Besides, we'll just put on a tiny bit. It will look fancy yet tasteful."

"Okay," said Claudia. "I'll do yours and you do mine."

I sat on the stool in the bathroom while Claudia applied my makeup.

"Now close your eyes," said Claudia as she swept some lavender eye shadow across my lids. "Keep them closed and roll your eyeballs back and forth."

"Does that help with the eye shadow?"

"No," said Claudia. "I just think it looks cool to see your eyeballs wiggle under your skin. There, I'm done! What do you think?"

I turned around and looked in the mirror.

"Oh my glaciers, Claudia, I love it!"

After I applied Claudia's makeup, we
both got dressed in our nice outfits.
Purple for me, and turquoise for her.
Diary, we looked smashing. But comfort?
That was another story.

"How's your dress feel?" I asked
Claudia.

Claudia had a big stiff smile on her face. "Oh, spectacular. How does *yours* feel?"

"Oh, *spectacular*," I said. "I wish I could wear this every day."

Claudia raised an eyebrow. "It's itchy, isn't it?"

"So itchy!" I hitched up my skirt and scratched my legs. "This one is even worse than the dress last night!"

"We can't cut the petticoats out this time because you can see them," said Claudia.

"No, and my mom would ground me forever," I said. "But we don't want to be scratching all through the wedding either. I know!" I ran to our suitcases.

"We'll use our favorite slippery slime-making ingredient: cornstarch!"

Luckily, Claudia and I don't travel anywhere without bringing cornstarch. You never know when you'll need to whip up a batch of slime.

"We'll sprinkle it all over our legs, and the itchy petticoats will slip and glide with ease."

"Lina, you are a genius."

We lifted up our skirts and sprinkled cornstarch on our legs. The dresses were still so itchy, though, so we added more. In the end, we decided that since we'd have to be in these dresses for hours, we'd better use the whole jar.

After that, we had a sneezing fit. Then we hitched up our skirts and flopped onto our beds to wait.

Diary, it is nine o'clock in the morning and we are dressed and ready to go. So far, so smooth.

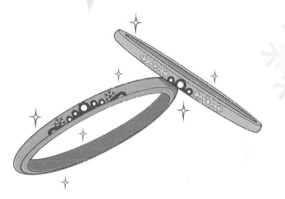

SMOOTH AS ROCKY ROAD

About an hour later, we heard a knock at the bedroom door.

It was my cousin Jack. He was dressed in a tuxedo that looked even itchier than our dresses. Sadly, we were all out of cornstarch.

"Hey, Lina, your mom sent me to

ask you—whoa." Jack leaned in closer to my face. "Are you supposed to look like that?"

"Of course I am. This is fancy yet tasteful. Now what did Mom say?"

"She asked me to come get you. They need someone to run messages back and forth from the kitchen."

"Oh, you mean they need Communications Officers! Coming right away!"

Claudia and I slipped on our nice shoes and hurried (as fast as you can in nice shoes) to the study, where my mom and dad were working on the flower bouquets.

"Oh good, Lina and Claudia, we need you to—whoa." My mom leaned in closer to my face. "Lina, what is all over your face?"

"It's fancy yet taste—"

"Young lady, you are going to have to wash that off before the wedding starts, is that clear? And what in the skies is all that out in the hall?"

We leaned out the parlor door. Puffy white clouds of powder floated in the air where we had been walking.

"Ooh," said Claudia. "We may have overdone it just a teensy bit with the cornstarch . . ."

My dad patted my mom's shoulder
and said, "Don't worry. I'll get to work
on cleaning it up."

After he left, I said, "Mom, I'm
sorry. We were just trying to make sure
everything went fine."

She sighed and smiled. "I know, sweetie. I'm just frustrated with these flowers. My powers are bringing the spring rains that make flowers *grow*, not making bouquets! I need to ask Aunt Eastia if these are good enough."

Claudia and I snapped to attention

and saluted. "Did someone order a pair of Communications Officers?"

Mom smiled. "Yes, that's exactly what I need! I think your great-aunt is down in the kitchen helping Chef Rehan."

We took the flowers downstairs and saw people swarming around the kitchen. We found Granddad there, fanning Great-Aunt Eastia, who looked on the verge of passing out.

"What's going on?" I asked.

"Disaster, disaster!" murmured Great-Aunt Eastia.

"CHEF REHAN TOOK THE WEDDING CAKE ONTO THE BALCONY FOR THE

**RECEPTION AND IT COLLAPSED ONTO
THE REST OF THE FOOD! THE WEDDING
FEAST IS COVERED IN GOOEY ICING!"**

My heart sank into my shoes. The
snow I made must have melted. That
beautiful cake—ruined.

Great-Aunt Eastia waved me over to her. "Deliver a message to Wendy. Tell her to start getting dressed and I will be up shortly to help her with the shoes."

Claudia took the flowers from me. "You go help your cousin. I'll take care of this."

Right. Everything was going smoothly.

Smooth as rocky road ice cream.

13

IF THE SHOE FITS

I ran down the hall, leaving a trail of
cornstarch behind me. I whispered to
myself, "Everything is fine, everything is
fine, everything is fine . . ."

Finally, I found Wendy's bedroom
and knocked on the door. "Hello?" I
called.

I opened the door and went inside. "Wendy? It's Lina."

The room was empty. Wendy's wedding dress was hanging on a stand near the window. I knew I wasn't supposed to see it before the wedding, but I just had to get a closer look.

Gosh, Diary, I have never seen something so pretty. Tiny gold flowers were embroidered all over it, with delicate little crystals sewn on top. It glittered like a diamond. I took a step back to admire it in the light, and that's when I tripped.

And then I fell.

And then I knocked over the chair.

And then I heard the worst sound I could imagine.

A glassy crunch.

I lifted the chair and set it aside. Underneath were Wendy's glass slippers.

What was left of them, anyway. The chair had crushed them into shards.

Well, Diary, what else could I do?

I flopped down on the ground and started bawling my eyes out.

14

COUSIN TO COUSIN

I must have been sobbing so hard that I didn't hear the bedroom door open.

"Lina, is that you?"

I looked up and saw Wendy dressed in her bathrobe and fuzzy slippers. The sight of her made me sob even harder.

She rushed to me and put her arm

around me. "Lina, don't cry, it's going to be—whoa." She held my face in her hands. "Your makeup, it's . . ."

"I know, it's awful!" I sobbed. "It was supposed to be fancy yet tasteful, but I guess we got carried away." I waved at the ring of white powder on the carpet. "Same with the cornstarch."

Wendy smiled. "It's not awful. It got smudged from your tears, but we can fix that."

She brought a wet washcloth from the bathroom and wiped the makeup off. "There," she said. "Now, that's perfect."

"No, not perfect," I sniffled. I took a

deep breath so I wouldn't start bawling again. "Oh, Wendy, I am so sorry . . . I crushed your wedding shoes! They're ruined and this is all my fault!"

She held my hands in hers. "Lina, you did not break those shoes. I did."

I snorted some snot back up into my nose. "Wait—you did?"

She nodded. "I was practicing dancing in them last night and I cracked them. Then I got really frustrated and I may have accidentally smashed them into pieces on purpose."

I gasped. "You did that?"

"Do you know how ridiculous glass slippers are? Super ridiculous!"

"Wendy, it's not just the shoes," I said. "I also let Gusty out of my room and he ate almost half of your wedding cake. And then I tried to cover it up by filling it in with snow, and then the snow melted, and . . . well, let's just say that the entire wedding is a disaster because of me. I wanted to help your day go perfectly smoothly, but I messed it all up."

Wendy flopped down on the ground beside me. "That's just the problem—trying to make everything perfect. The whole family has been running around, stressed about things that don't really matter to us. I don't even like One Thousand Almonds Cake—and Sunny is allergic to almonds! I have always hated those glass shoes because I can't dance in them, and dancing is the best part about a wedding. And my dress . . ."

"That dress is so beautiful," I said.

"Lina, that dress is the itchiest thing I have ever worn. I can't even look at it without scratching!"

I laughed. "I know exactly how you feel."

Wendy sighed. "I wish I could tell Eastia and Granddad, but they're working so hard to put this wedding together. They'll be so disappointed if Sunny and I tell them it's not what we want."

But, Diary, would they really?

I felt like Great-Aunt Sunder's letter had made everyone think they had to do things a certain way. But I knew that deep down what they wanted most of all was for Wendy to be happy. She didn't look happy at all right then.

There was a knock at the door, and Claudia and Jack opened it.

"Lina, we've been looking everywhere for you!" said Claudia.

"And, Wendy, thank goodness you're

here," said Jack. "The wedding is supposed to start in one hour!"

I stood up and dusted the cornstarch off my dress. Then I helped my cousin to her feet. "Wendy, we are going to make sure you have the perfect day—perfect for *you and Sunny.*"

I motioned to Claudia and Jack. "These two will assist you in the fashion department." I pointed to Wendy's wedding dress. "Guys, this needs some work."

"I can already tell that dress is itchier than an ant bite," said Claudia. "Give me some scissors and I'm on it."

"I think I can add a few artistic touches," said Jack.

I smiled. "Wendy, you're in good
hands. I'll be back soon."

"Where are you going?"

"To communicate."

TOUGH TALK

It wasn't easy to gather my family together in Granddad's library, but somehow I managed to convince them to give me two minutes of their time.

"Lina, can't this wait until after the wedding?" asked my mom. "I still have to finish the flowers."

"AND I HAVE TO PREPARE MY SPEECH," said Granddad. **"MY JOKES STILL NEED WORK!"**

Great-Aunt Eastia buried her face in her hands. "Oh, this wedding is not at all how it should be. If Sunder were here, she'd laugh in our faces."

"But that's just the problem," I said. "You are all working so hard to impress Great-Aunt Sunder and she's not even here! And even if she was, why should we care about what she thinks? All that matters is that Wendy and Sunny are happy, right?"

Then—like the good Communications Officer I am—I told them how Wendy

and Sunny just wanted a simple wedding with all the family there to celebrate with them. I explained that they appreciated all the work everyone was doing, but they didn't need all the fancy stuff to make them happy.

When I was done communicating, my family sat around nodding.

"I can grow Wendy and Sunny a whole meadow of pretty flowers—and it will be much nicer than the ones I put in a vase," said my mom.

Great-Aunt Eastia threw her hands up. "I don't really care where anyone sits, to be honest."

"AND I HATE PUBLIC SPEAKING!" shouted Granddad.

We all laughed. It felt so nice to finally see my family relaxed and smiling.

My dad put his arm around me. "It

sounds like you got everyone on the same page, Lina. So now what do you think we should do? We still have a wedding to put on."

I thought for a long moment.

"I think I have an idea," I said. "But

everyone in the family is going to need to pitch in."

Great-Aunt Eastia smiled at me. "Lina, we are ready for you to put us to work."

16

A WEDDING TO REMEMBER

The wedding started two hours late, which meant we were just in time for the most glorious sunset I have ever seen.

Wendy and Sunny were married outside, on a fluffy field of pink-and-golden clouds. My mom and the

Skypainters in our family decorated
the sky with rainbows. My great-aunt
Eastia blew in a sweet, warm breeze. My
great-uncle Weston strummed a song
on his guitar.

The bride wore a simple dress that
was not even the tiniest bit itchy (thanks
to Claudia). Her hair was decorated with

glittering designs of frosted crystals (thanks to Jack). And she didn't wear any shoes at all.

Now I am not a mushy person, Diary, but I did smile when the Sparkarchers in our family made lightning bolts when the bride and groom kissed.

The best part, though? Granddad cried big happy tears through the whole thing.

When the ceremony was over, Wendy scooped me into a giant hug. "Oh, Lina, that was just what we wanted! Thank you so much for making it happen."

I hugged her back. "It was the perfect wedding."

"*Was?*" She winked at me and Claudia. "This wedding is just getting started."

17

WE ARE FAMILY

✳ SUNDAY ✳

Diary, I never knew my family could party that hard.

After the ceremony, we all went inside Granddad's castle for dinner. Everyone sat wherever they wanted. Chef Rehan had prepared a last-minute feast: the yummiest sandwiches I have ever tasted.

He also whipped up a whole batch of wedding cupcakes that he arranged in a spiral tower. Even Gusty was allowed to have one!

Granddad did give a speech—but not a cheesy speech with canned jokes. He spoke from the heart about how much he loved Wendy and Sunny and all of us. That made *everyone* cry.

Then we all kicked off our shoes and danced until the break of dawn to Claudia's perfect playlist. I will say this about my relatives: They know how to *boogie*.

Halfway through the night, Great-Aunt Eastia gave me permission to lay down a sheet of ice on the dance floor. Wendy and Sunny led us in a slip-slide-swirl-a-thon!

"Now *this* is what I call a perfectly
smooth evening!" said Jack, sliding
past me.

Claudia and I hooked arms and
twirled around in a circle. "I think this
will be remembered as the wedding of
the century!" she said.

"Even better," I said. "The wedding of
the millennium!"

COLORFUL ICE SCULPTURES!

Use the science of salt and melting ice to create lovely colorful sculptures!

MATERIALS:

* Plastic bowls, dishes, or water balloons
* Table salt
* Food coloring or liquid watercolor
* Medicine dropper or pipette
* Medicine dropper or pipette
* Baking tray with a rim
* Food thermometer (optional)
* A grown-up assistant

START SCULPTING:

First, make sure you have a clean, dry work space. You may want to cover your surface with paper towels or a plastic tablecloth to protect it. Any spills can be cleaned up with soap and water.

The night before you start your experiment, fill the bowls or water balloons with tap water and put them in the freezer. Have your grown-up assistant help you with this. When the water has frozen solid, take the ice out of the containers and place it on the baking tray. The tray will help contain the mess as the ice melts!

Take some time to notice the texture and appearance of your ice. Is it smooth or bumpy? Are there bubbles inside? Next, sprinkle some salt on top of the ice. Now what do you notice?

SALT SCIENCE:

If you put your ice sculpture onto the tray without any salt, it would melt fairly slowly because some of the melting water would refreeze on the surface of the ice. But when you sprinkle salt on top, it mixes with the melting water and lowers the freezing temperature of the water. This means that the water must get much colder to refreeze. The salty water will continue melting the ice, forming the cracks and patterns that you see.

KEEP GOING:

Now use a dropper or pipette to add some food coloring to the ice sculpture. The color will flow into the cracks and valleys formed by the salty water, creating beautiful patterns.

This experiment can go in so many interesting directions. You could set a challenge for yourself (*Can we use the salt to carve a hole all the way through the ice?*). Or you could take some data with the thermometer (*What is the temperature of the ice with and without salt?*). Or you could go with the flow and create lovely ice decorations fit for a royal Windtamer wedding!

Be cool-not warm-and read some of Lina's first adventure!

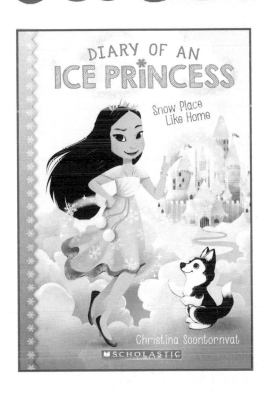

DIARY OF AN ICE PRINCESS

Snow Place Like Home

Christina Soontornvat

SCHOLASTIC

THE NIGHT BEFORE THE BIG DAY

✳ FRIDAY ✳

Tonight is the perfect night to start a new diary because there is no way I can fall asleep!

Tomorrow is our family picnic. Why am I so excited, Diary? It's just a normal, old family picnic, right?

Except our picnic is in the clouds.

And our family is definitely *not* normal.

I just triple-checked all my stuff for tomorrow:

Lucky socks ✓

Lucky purple tiara ✓

Lucky dress (the only one
I have that isn't ripped!) ✓

Oh my glaciers, Diary!

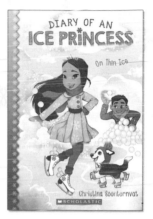

Princess Lina is the *coolest* girl in school!

■SCHOLASTIC

scholastic.com

DIARYICEPRINCESS5

CHRISTINA SOONTORNVAT grew up behind the counter of her parents' Thai restaurant, reading stories. These days she loves to make up her own, especially if they involve magic. Christina also loves science and worked in a science museum for years before pursuing her dream of being an author. She still enjoys cooking up science experiments at home with her two young daughters. You can learn more about Christina and her books on her website at soontornvat.com.